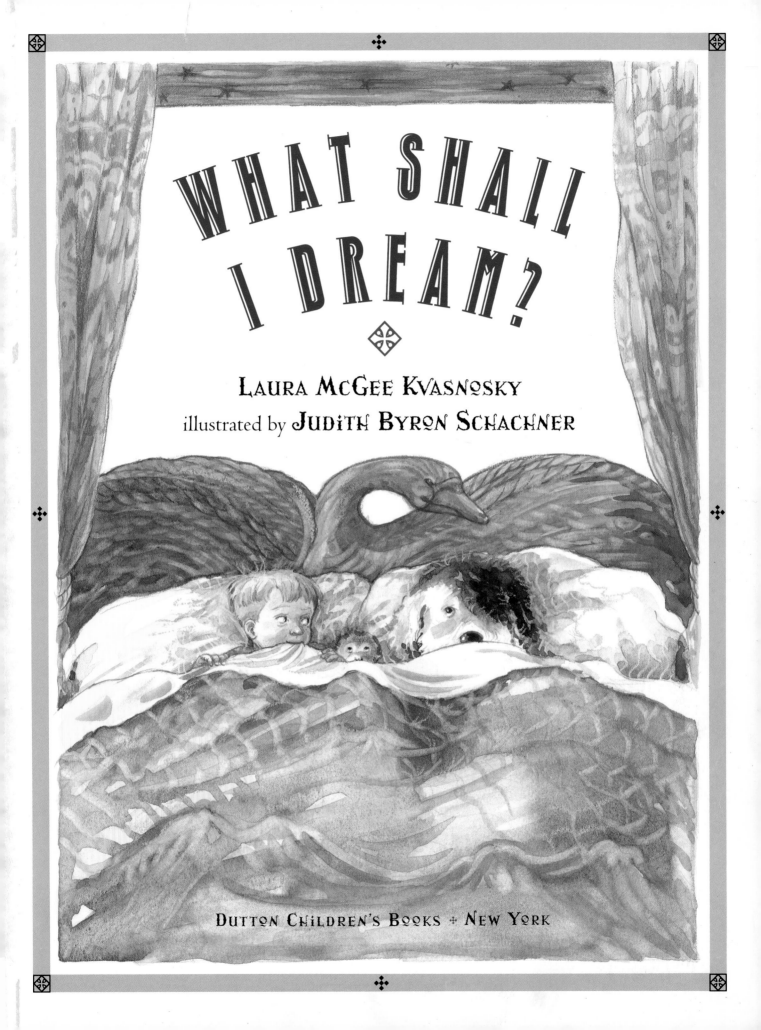

WHAT SHALL I DREAM?

Laura McGee Kvasnosky

illustrated by Judith Byron Schachner

Dutton Children's Books · New York

Library of Congress Cataloging-in-Publication Data

Kvasnosky, Laura McGee.
What shall I dream? / by Laura McGee Kvasnosky:
illustrated by Judith Byron Schachner.—1st ed.
p. cm.
Summary: Despite the well-intentioned efforts of the King,
Queen, and others, only Prince Alexander can find the dreams
that are right for him.
ISBN 0-525-45207-9 (hardback)
[1. Dreams—Fiction. 2. Princes—Fiction.]
I. Schachner, Judith Byron, ill. II. Title.
PZ7.K975Wh 1996 [E]—dc20 95-30890 CIP AC

Published in the United States 1996 by Dutton Children's Books,
a division of Penguin Books USA Inc.
375 Hudson Street, New York, New York 10014

Designed by Amy Berniker
Printed in Hong Kong
First Edition
1 3 5 7 9 10 8 6 4 2

For John, who shares my dreams,
and Nancy, who reminds me dreams come true

L.M.K.

To Sir Bob, with love

J.B.S.

So the Queen rushed the best riders on their fastest horses to the cliffs above the sea. There they found the Dream Weavers casting seamless dreams out across the kingdom. The Weavers, too, were glad to help the young Prince, and they loaded their stuff of dreams into glimmering nets and hurried to the castle.

The great castle was quiet as the King tucked his little boy into bed.

"Good night, sleep tight, don't let the fleas bite," the King said.

Prince Alexander snuggled closer to his dog, Winnie. But he didn't go right to sleep. "Daddy," he asked, "what shall I dream?"

"Ah," said the King, "what to dream?" The King sat down on the bed. "This is a serious matter, my son. Let us consult the experts. I will send for the Dream Brewers to brew you a kingly dream."

So the King rushed his best riders on their fastest horses to the River of Stars.

There they found the tiny Brewers stirring their dreamy blend as it wafted out across the kingdom. The Brewers were half asleep from working over their steamy cups, but they roused themselves and loaded their rickety cart with the stuff of dreams and headed toward the castle.

By the time they arrived, it was well past the Prince's bedtime. The Brewers went right to work. Humming softly, they mixed up granite chips, gold coins, and a splash of river water. Soon a heavy goo bubbled in the bottom of the cup, and a cloud billowed over the brim.

Alexander nodded to one side. He nodded to the other. The fog of dreams soon filled his head.

He dreamed he was King, sitting on a throne in a Great Hall. Piles of money and stacks of papers surrounded him. A long line of petitioners waited to talk to him.

All he could do was work, work, work: counting money, signing papers, settling matters of state. It wasn't fun. He wasn't happy.

When Alexander awoke the next morning, he was not rested.

"That might be a good dream for a king," he told his dog, Winnie.

"But it isn't the right dream for me."

All day, Alexander tried to figure out what to dream. While playing croquet on the East Lawn, he asked the gardener, "What shall I dream?"

"Perhaps a dream of roses," the gardener suggested.

While making mud pies in the castle kitchen, Alexander asked the cook, "What shall I dream?"

"Why not a dream of savory partridge stew?" the cook proposed.

Neither of these answers seemed quite right to Alexander, so he asked Winnie. Unfortunately, though, animals are apt to keep their thoughts to themselves.

By day's end, Prince Alexander still had no answer.

"Mama," he sighed as he was getting ready for bed, "how can I get a good sleep? I don't know what to dream."

"Ah," said the Queen, "we just need to find the right experts. Let's ask the Dream Weavers to fashion you a perfect dream."

When they arrived, they assembled a hundred looms. The Prince was very tired by the time it was all ready. "What shall I dream? What shall I dream?" he grumped.

The Weavers went right to work. They wove lace and feathers and velvet streaked with silver among their threads. A hundred shuttles flew as the huge dream tapestry took shape.

Prince Alexander nodded to one side. He nodded to the other. Sleep covered him like soft wool.

He dreamed that he stood in a room lined with mirrors. Tailors were fitting him into a velvet suit. "Stand still," said one tailor. "Yes, just a nip here at the waist and a touch more stiffness in the collar."

Alexander squealed. "Oh," said another tailor, "sorry about that pin."

"This suit is too tight, and this crown hurts my head," complained Alexander. But no one listened.

When he awoke the next morning, he was even less rested than before.

"That might be a good dream for a queen," he said to Winnie, "but it isn't the right dream for me."

That day, Alexander searched through books in the Royal Library for dream ideas. But he had no luck.

When his grandfather came to tuck him into bed, Alexander was in tears. "What shall I dream?" he sobbed. "I'll never get a good sleep if I don't know what to dream."

"Ah," said his grandfather, "we must consult the experts. Let's send for the Dream Sweepers to whirl you a fine dream."

So the riders were sent off again, this time to the high desert. There they found the Dream Sweepers whisking dreamy dust out across the kingdom. The Sweepers packed their stuff of dreams onto camels and hurried to the castle.

When they arrived, Alexander was so cross he was hiding in a lump under the covers. Quickly, the Sweepers scattered sparkling sand and a sprinkle of silver scales. Their piper played a sweet tune as they began to sweep.

The powders swirled and dashed and drifted down on the lump that was Alexander. He nodded to one side. He nodded to the other. The dust of dreams soon filled his head.

He dreamed he fished in a quiet oasis. He cast his line and waited for a bite. Deep in the dark green water, the silver glint of a lunker caught Alexander's eye. But the fish ignored his bait. Afternoon turned to evening as Alexander waited without even a nibble. B-O-R-I-N-G, he thought.

When he awoke, he told Winnie, "That might be a good dream for a grandfather, but it isn't the right dream for me."

By this time, Prince Alexander was more worried than ever about what to dream.

He thought about it while sailing on the South Pond.

He fussed about it during tea on the West Lawn.

He fretted about it as he walked down to feed the swans with his nursemaid, Henrietta.

Now Alexander was very tired from not getting a good sleep for three nights. As he and Henrietta sat on the shore watching the swans, he rested his head on her lap.

Sleepily, he asked her, "What shall I dream?"

And quietly, she answered, "Sweet Prince, you must discover your dreams yourself. Close your eyes. You will find them."

Before she could even finish speaking, Alexander nodded to one side. He nodded to the other. He settled into a warm nest of sleep.

And he dreamed.

He dreamed of sailing the ocean blue, dancing wild jigs with Winnie and the sailors, singing sea chanties at the top of his voice. Then Winnie climbed to the crow's nest and called down, "Land ho!"

He dreamed of eating a sumptuous tea on a sunny terrace. There were raspberry scones and peanut butter finger sandwiches and a chocolate cake as tall as he could reach. Henrietta passed the cream and sugar. "Three lumps, please," said Winnie.

And he dreamed of riding a swan high above the kingdom, swooping from the River of Stars to the sea cliffs to the high desert and back again to the castle. "One more time," shouted Winnie as they came in for a landing.

When Alexander awoke, he was looking straight up at a huge swan. But instead of crying out, he sat up and smiled.

From that time on, he dreamed his own dreams. They were simply magnificent, and they suited him exactly.